Fandanzel

A Haunting Tale in the Forest

Written and Illustrated by
Sarah McNaught

www.sarahmcnaught.com

First published 2012 by

www.fast-print.net/store.php

Fandanzel – A Haunting Tale in the Forest
Copyright © Sarah McNaught 2012

ISBN 978-178035-299-2

Cover art design by: Steven McNaught Interaktiv Design
www.interaktiv.com.au

An environmentally friendly book printed and bound in
England by www.printondemand-worldwide.com

This book is made entirely of chain-of-custody materials

Preface

Revisit your childhood with this enchanting tale, for old and young alike. Make a cup of cocoa, crack open the shortbread and read this yourself; then read it to the children.

Fandanzel is created to raise awareness amongst young and old readers alike, of nature and the countryside in a creative way, taking them on a journey that is factual and explanative, but fictionally exciting, with lots of focus on the haunting mystery of nature.

The characters are born out of real life observations, but with a very different twist to the norm. This story offers the reader a most enchanting viewpoint on life in the countryside, around the villages of Langley, Forest

Chapel and Sutton in Cheshire, and the majesty of the surrounding forest and moors.

Fandanzel is set on the border of Cheshire and Derbyshire, stretching from the hills of the Pennines to the Cheshire Plain, in The Peak District National Park. The land that is now the park itself dates back as far as the 11th century with ancient woodlands and quarries. The majesty of its glory and the people associated with the running of it inspired me with this story. 'Fandanzel' is a fox but not just any old fox. He is a pioneer, almost human in fact. Come with me, meet his friends and help him survive adventures that evolve throughout a year in time.

JANUARY –
THE EVE OF ROBBIE BURNS

Serena was still. Nevertheless, Serena, the placid reservoir, was always like that, home to birds such as the Grebes and Coots, the fish known to humans as Pike and Trout. However, tonight Serena was angry and the ice that bound her was getting irksome. She was calm, yet unhappy thinking hard about days of basking in the summer sun with tourists admiring her form, since 1850.

Fandanzel shuddered sitting by the steps on that bitterly cold January night, not from the icy chill, but anticipation that he would have to cross Serena's snowbound surface. He was a scavenger and needed by instinct to scurry in hunt of food across her back, but the rumble and crack, that came from what seemed like the bowels of the earth, worried him. The sound was like that of a huge whale trapped beneath her surface. He had scampered down the dozen slippery steps then huddled under 'Little Tree's' deep brown and grey twisted winter branches, and thought hard about his mission.

He was a strong and cunning fox, well-bred and from a long line of extremely good survivors, but this situation with Serena worried him. This eerie noise sounded like the centre of the earth moaning in protest against the cruelty of winter.

For winter was a long and difficult time. The livestock and their keepers struggled to farm the land against the savage wind and cold.

The ponies felt left behind by their rider friends that breezed in and out for parties from the riding school in summer, when everyone sought out the warmth of shops and sat in front of computer aided packages in the winter days.

They forgot that the Strawberry Roan, Bay Mare and Piebald Pony needed love and regular exercise. They required cleaning, new shoes; new feed and frequent brushing, but thanks to the dedicated stable-hands, the umpteen horses at the stables were impeccably looked after.

Back at the reservoir there was nothing else for it; Fandanzel had to cross the ice to get back to the den where he could at last be protected against the bitter chill.

Boldly he scurried in a zigzag pattern down the embankment

towards the huge wall that encased Serena, it's depth was amazingly thick and almost infinite, to hold the immense pressure that the water created against the bank.

Fandanzel had been told that dry stone walls dated back to the 18th century and even into medieval times. They were used in the North of England as dividing walls by the ancient settlers and farmers to retain their livestock. Yet the wall that encased Serena was solid reinforced concrete, a stark contrast in an ageless landscape.

He was nearly half way across the stretch of frozen water and again came the noise, louder this time and longer. It seemed to be coming at him from every direction, and he ran, faster and faster, his heart pounding in his tawny chest. Keep running, keep running, and keep running, he told himself.

An earsplitting crack, like that of a huge piece of glass being shattered, shook him and he toppled over skidding to a petrified halt. His breath came quickly and caused a steady mist in the night air.

Then slowly it came to him. The reservoir was thawing, the day had been less cold and the sun had shone. Serena was about to crack and he was on the very top of where she was about to split open her icy depths.

Luckily for Fandanzel, after what seemed like an age, he escaped to the shallow safety of the old reed bed where he shook himself over and over again, trembling with fear and gasping for air.

In the stillness of the night, he heard the festivities still going at the nearby tavern, celebrating the birthday of the much-loved poet, Robbie Burns born this day 25th January 1759.

The locals were cheering in the kilt-clad Scotsman, with their clapping, and the distinctive mellow tone of bagpipes could be heard throughout the forest. The haggis, traditionally served with potatoes and turnips was about to be eaten.

Besides the roaring fires of the public house, stories of olden times were being told.

Far away in some place called "a mile-a-way" according to humans, apparently, there was another reservoir, made in 1929, yet not as calm as Serena.

This faraway place was Trentabank. This reservoir was bigger, bolder and with an overflow that let out thousands of gallons of water daily in February, when the rains came and made an amazing spectacle.

However Fandanzel was not so impressed because the concrete bottom of the manmade waterfall was slick and greenish, making it slippery for him to cross it. He was too tired to think and so, for a while, lay beneath the silver birches, taking shelter and enjoying comfort from the awesomely strong wind, behind a dry stone wall.

"Fox, Fox, Foooooox", whispered the voice "Fox, Fox, Fandanzel", it came again.

"You need to take great care if you want to live to see another Burn's Night", and then the voice was gone.

It was almost as though the old oak tree, planted in 1931, along with over two and a half thousand more, Fandanzel was leaning against, was breathing. In and out, then again, in, out, in, out.

The wind must be making noises in my head, he decided shaking his ears. However, he was very wrong, for Fandanzel was resting beneath the protective oaken trunk of 'Little Wide Tree's winter form, her voice whispering the words to him nervously.

"You live to see another day little fox" came a man's voice from behind, and Fandanzel turned to faintly see the ghost of Robbie Burns melting into the night. Robbie and Fandanzel had met before in another lifetime,

"maybe next year you will not be so fast and lucky". Fandanzel slowly realised that his master had come to warn him from the dead.

Huddled and shivering nervously at any slight noise, 'Little Wide Tree' may have looked bare and ugly, but she calmed the fox with her whispering as the wind raged through her very soul.

She looked like any other winter tree, but with a root ball that was similar to the face of a garlic bulb, she swayed and arched against the gusts that were coming from the east side of The Pennines.

By morning, Serena seemed not as scary. Fandanzel saw that the measuring stick marker that usually dictated her water level was set upon by a large rook.

That meant the water level had dropped for some reason; possibly the reservoir was being released. However he did not have time to ponder this now. The bird quickly headed skywards, alarmed by something.

Fandanzel's limbs responded to the birds own adrenalin by a sharp tingle that meant flight or fight; he knew that feeling well.

It began as a distant howling in the forest. Quickly it came closer: until suddenly Fandanzel was confronted with a breathtaking sight completely unexpected. A six pack of gleaming white dogs, blood red tongues flopping beneath foaming jowls, bared teeth yellow in the whiteness of the contrasting snow.

Their ears were pinned back and then came another sound, dull thudding almost wheel-like, spinning, skidding. There behind their pulling reins was a miniature Roman chariot driven by a wild haired man of great strength and heading at least twenty miles per hour to exactly where Fandanzel huddled stricken numb by fear.

The rook had long flapped his wings and was already heading away at speed.

Daylight had barely broken over the Sitka pines when a torch-like vision emerged from the rear of the chariot.

Fandanzel had never seen anything like it in his life, not here in these well- trodden paths of the earth that he claimed as his. The animals that towed the chariot emerged like a leaping, straining, howling force of nature.

Then they were gone... as quickly as they had come.

2.

Above the wood-burning stove at the cottage in Langley, sat upon an oak mantle, carved in 1854 from a fallen tree, caught in a savage storm at the foot of Tegg's Nose park and positioned with pride, was a brass Portuguese style clock that James' parents had brought back from holidays years ago.

He had not even been born then and so the clock seemed almost antique to his tender eight years. One second, two seconds, ten seconds, twenty, then five minutes had passed. Ten frustratingly went to twenty and by thirty five, Alex; his best friend was late almost beyond being bearable.

As James paced the window for the umpteenth time that icy morning he noticed the beads of condensation running down the tiny panes of the old Georgian window, behind them a dusty scattering of snow shimmered like silver dust lit by the watery early morning sun.

He hastily plucked an orange from the fruit bowl on the dining table and began to peel it. James had already phoned the child-minder the evening before, when his parents were finishing their supper, to explain untruthfully, that his mother would be taking the day off tomorrow.

Also that they wouldn't need her to look after him after all... and that she was so sorry that she couldn't make the call herself, but there was a problem with the dishwasher flooding.

This was such a most convincing lie that Trish accepted it, and even offered James the phone number of a reliable plumber and passed on her hopes that it got fixed quickly. James was not usually deceptive.

"Come on Alex, where are you? We should have left ages ago, it's nearly nine, you're always late" muttered James to himself frowning and adjusting the straps of the sixty litre backpack he had snuck out of the shed yesterday, for another final check. His father had taught him well as a Scout leader to check his equipment and make sure that he would be prepared for adventure.

If Alex would finally turn up, they could start their planned day at the Forest and be back, changed, and in front of the TV before anyone would know that they had been out.

Not that they had been unaccompanied on a 13km trek, around the Peak District National Park, looking for alleged ghosts of poachers, in the inky black stillness of the silent thickets of swaying spruces.

A deafening yelp violently shook James, he spun around to the adjacent hall door, and it finished with a whine, a whimper and again this time a ferocious bark.

James' heart pounded, his hands shook as he fumbled with the Yale lock holding the collar of the muscular black Labrador that was by now on two legs hoping for a glimpse of the intruder behind the glass.

"Get down, get down Berry, come on, it's only Alex, he's been here millions of times". James tugged at the door that had swollen with unusually damp weather over Christmas. It wasn't damp now.

The air was clear, the sky topaz blue and the hills outside beckoning. "Where've you been all this time, we agreed eight thirty, what are you wearing trainers for, you know we'll never get over Shutlingsloe Hill with you wearing those", chuckled James. "Quick! Come in." Alex hopped into the tiny hall of the cottage and grinned. His face was red and cold, his breathing quick as he explained to James.

"I had to walk. Dad would have suspected something if I'd asked for a lift". James clipped on Berry's lead and patted her "Good girl" he soothed, "Good dog" as his friend hastily drank from a packed flask with satisfying gulps to a boy that had virtually run all the way to James' house.

So, on a brisk morning before the eve of Burn's Night, an average Saturday whilst James' parents were working at the hotel and golf club, the two friends, one black dog and ample provisions headed off on a boys' crusade and mission to prove that they could go it alone into the world.

They would be back to help with the preparation for the festivities planned for the celebration of Robert Burn's birthday who died in 1796. James' mother had told him that he had been a famous poet.

It was a busy time at the club and associated hotel; they would be busy setting up the dance floor and the tables. James told Alex not to worry so much, no-one would even notice.

"You'll see, trust me. Now get the map and compass out, you set it" continued James.

Steadily climbing the Gritstone Trail at the base of Tegg's Nose, a gritstone escarpment rising six hundred feet above the four reservoirs, Berry in tow, the boys chatted and laughed over schoolboy anecdotes as they hiked in step with each other, they had done treks like these many times with Cubs and would soon be Scouts.

Back in the late 19th Century, the gritstone was quarried to be used for making the paving slabs and roofing tiles for the nearby town of Macclesfield, and beyond. Its geological composition was ideal for stone with its millstone grits at the upper end and bed of shale between each gritstone layer.

The latter grit was cut off from the others by Red Rock fault at the valley and that was where the boys were heading ready to turn right at the tree known as 'Old Gnarly' to climb the northern route that twined over a trail to the top leading to the quarry.

Alex enjoyed school, especially history. James was more into geography and the two of them were a good combination.

"Mr.Clowes told me that in 1878 there were some workers at the reservoir and one hit something by accident with his axe and it turned out not to be a pipe as they all thought, but guess what?" asked Alex eagerly.

"Dunno errrm! Some precious rock maybe? Tell me go on", answered James.

"Bones! Human bones, how cool is that?" Berry's ears cocked and she stared at Alex, as he repeated the word bones.

"Wicked! Answered James, turning his gaze from the map that he had been tracking as his father had taught him.

"Yeah! There was an urn dating back to Celtic times with young human bones and an arrowhead. Don't understand what it was doing there though, "stated Alex as he skidded upon the glasslike puddles that pitted the path. His trainers having no grip meant that Alex was to struggle for the rest of the day.

As the boys' backpacks started to feel very heavy after walking steadily North East, they took rest at the top of Tegg's Nose on one of the picnic benches in the newly created quarry Visitor Centre and took elevenses.

Hot blackcurrant cordial and jam tarts were shared whilst they regained their lost bearings from a study of the Ordnance Survey map neatly concertinaed, and protected from moisture in a clear plastic wallet on a red nylon cord.

Alex stretched and arched his back to regain his posture, heaved the backpack upwards, and clipped the straps. James followed suit placing the map carefully around his neck, and zipping up his coat, shivered and looked around the gloomy highly chiseled cliffs at his sides.

"Must have been spooky working up here mate don't you think all those years ago". James exclaimed shivering violently. "Let's get out of here". He briskly suggested to Alex feeling a little panic coming over him, but not wanting to perturb his friend. Eyes down, and with a swift stride, he set off quickly glancing over his shoulder to ensure that Alex was following, which he was, all but a stride or two to James' left side, chattering.

Suddenly, Alex's voice abruptly ceased, and there was a loud bump followed by the sound of shingle or some sort of small rocks falling down the side of the path. Shortly afterwards hurtling out of control were clumps of pinkish rock covered in black heather.

"What was that?" gasped James. "Alex, Alex, Alex" he shouted, "where are you, Alex?" Within a minute Alex popped up from a short distance down the hill.

"You were right, these trainers are rubbish for this sort of walk", smiled Alex sheepishly, "I just skidded all the way down there, look", pointed the boy.

"You had me going there for a bit" said James. "Come on! You all right though? Not broken anything have you?" Alex straightened up looking solemn as he turned his gaze quickly to where he had emerged.

"It's Berry, she skidded with me. She's not here mate, she's not here".

The boys raced to the edge. The dog had vanished.

3.

Like a ferry emerging from the fog of the English Channel, came forty or more of them. A gang of mixed ages, all male, all dressed strangely carrying pickaxes, shovels and sticks of dynamite.

Alex recognised the dress sense from his studies in History on the late Victorian workhouses and The Poor Law.

These men were bearded, some with moustaches, mostly wearing flat caps, waistcoats and sturdy boots, their sleeves rolled to the elbow.

Nobody in their right mind could possibly be running a themed quarrying party surely even the park's events management wasn't that creative.

This must be an apparition thought Alex, but did not feel like mentioning it to James with Berry missing and their nerves already taut.

The typical change in temperature associated with certain degrees above sea-level especially in January, had meant that the crispness felt with the earlier observed topaz blue sky in the village, evolved into a fog so thick suddenly, that not a hand could be seen in front of the boys' faces.

"Alex" exclaimed James, "Try the head torch; here; quickly we should be able to see better that way". James threw it to Alex panicking and fumbling for his own in his invisible backpack. It was the latter part of morning yet why did he feel so blind. His head was spinning.

For, what seemed like an age, there was silence; the 'pea-souper' feeling associated with claustrophobia, dizziness, disorientation and muted silence, all that could be heard by the boys was their respective heartbeats and heavy breathing. Beat, beat, beat, like the earlier sounding of the clock on the mantelpiece back at home, James could hear himself. Tick, tick, tick. They did not realise, due to the fog that they were only feet apart but it felt like a world.

The sound of multiple echoing chisels in the soupy haze became stronger along with a feeling of surreal abandonment.

"Take the top end and be quick, get the shaft prepared we're going to blast this one gentlemen" James heard a voice declare.

The two boys fled for their lives, skidding and scrambling at the embankment where Alex had only just ascended from minutes earlier. Berry had long gone and needed to be found.

As the boys' backpacks got heavier with the change from fog to penetrating rain, after an hour or so, torrents blasted, transported again later by clouds of freezing cloud.

The weather in that area often changed aggressively daily. It was moody, taunting and intense and sometimes wreaked havoc. Helicopters flew over the forest in search of fallen trees that posed problems to the power lines occasionally.

The mountain rescue number was periodically written throughout areas of the National Park on posters;

however the public tourists were unaware often of the powers of nature and the lifesaving information on the Ranger Station noticeboard was often overlooked, as people checked what time the tea and coffee van opening times were.

Alex drained the last of his flask.

"It's so cold James I can't feel my hands and feet" Alex weakly broke out between the chattering of his teeth and lips sore and cracked. "I can't make out where we are, I don't think we're anywhere near Shutlingsloe. The compass is pointing in the wrong direction, we should be going this way, look", Alex announced. James held out the plastic document holder between his sodden gloved hands, he too was feeling weak and disorientated.

The supplies in the backpacks had long since been consumed and the sun was heading down.

"The sun sets in the West doesn't it? Then if we line the compass up as we stand due North, look, we should have the setting sun on the other side almost" added Alex brightening a little.

The sky above cleared immediately and abruptly came a deafening audible inferno of geese, flapping gracefully in unison heading towards the setting sun in a V formation, the undersides of their pale grey abdomens becoming russet as they gained closer to the sun.

Then as quickly as they had arrived overhead, they were off into the January evening ahead.

"That's it!" James exclaimed and the two boys smiled as they read each of their friends' minds. "The geese are heading home for the night in the west. There's their sanctuary down the lane from our cottage. We need to follow them, quickly" continued James. "But, Berry, Berry, we have to keep looking for her" a tearful James added frustrated between doing the sensible thing and the loyalty to his trusty pet.

Alex and James stopped dead in their tracks. Heading towards them down a snow and ice covered lane came the sounds of several dogs advancing at speed, the whooshing sound of wheels and the yelling of a man. Into their spectrum came six or so husky dogs pulling what looked at first to be a Roman chariot, but with closer inspection it was glinting metallically holding a wild haired and enormous man with a beard.

"I've heard of this guy, he does this for a hobby". James told his friend. "I thought he was hunting foxes, I'd hate to be a fox if that was hurtling towards me with those dogs and him like a savage" spluttered Alex.

"He's the builder that did some work on our house, wave at him Alex, jump up and down, let's flag him down, surely he will have seen Berry". James shrieked, and so the two boys ran towards the encroaching vehicle that was travelling at over twenty miles an hour in their direction. The enormous savage looking man was Darl Baker.

Within an hour Darl had managed to revive the two explorers at his brother's Inn, the same hostelry that was due to hold a Burn's Night dance later. Soon enough the warmth and colour came back to them, as they sipped hot cock-a-leekie soup and dunked oatmeal bread with vigor. They rugged up in blankets by a roaring coal fire, at the side of which was a sleeping white and tan terrier. James became aware of the time and sadly of Berry.

"Cummon lads, let's get you both back to civilisation and home, I think a hot bath would be a good idea." Came Darl's almighty booming voice, Interrupting James' thoughts, and before too long they were bumping along the road downwards to Langley in the mighty man's truck. Darl explained that they would assume a search for the dog the following morning bright and early.

"Don't worry fellas, dogs can survive pretty OK as long as they stay dry and get water. I'll help ye both in the morn."

As the vehicle pulled up outside the unlit cottage, the boys thanked Darl and agreed that he'd collect them at 7am to begin the search. They wearily trudged into the hall after locating the key they had hidden under a rock by the frozen pond, beneath the hedge at the front of the cottage.

Then came a shuffling sound, something was hiding in the coal shed, the creature started to whimper, and erupted into a loud bark. The two boys raced to the shed, and there crouched in the corner, blacker than black, due to the coal dust, was Berry.

James and Alex flung their arms around her neck, and hugged the frightened animal until she ceased her shuddering.

"Oh Berry" laughed James, "I'm so glad you're not a yellow Labrador, I'd never get you clean after this". Alex joined in the laughter and wearily they all disappeared inside to warmth and shelter.

4.

Berry still shivered in her basket by the simmering log burner looking tired and worried. She had been spooked up at the quarry earlier in the day and by instinct, headed back to where she knew safety and shelter; and that was home.

Having taken a rough tumble down the face of Tegg's Nose through gorse bushes, and over remnants of stone, tipped over the edge well over a hundred years ago; she had suffered small grazes but nothing of significance. All the same she sure had witnessed more fun days previously.

The boys and Berry were soon comfortable in the cottage and with

the imminent return of James'
parents to deal with; they set about
cleaning up Berry's scratches, had
quick showers, and hastily fed
themselves and the dog. Then they
plonked down in front of the TV
exhausted.

Some time later, Alex having
departed when his father collected
him at eight, James cleaned and
dried the backpack he had snuck
belonging to his father.

He waited until the family was
quiet in the lounge, and he set about
returning it to the garden shed. As he
gingerly crept into the shed's doorway
ready to hang the article on the hook,
he sensed something.

Turning slowly, his back to the
muted prisms of light being cast
through the slatted blind in the
kitchen, there in half shadow, and

half lit by crystal moonshine, stood a fabulous fox.

For a moment boy and beast regarded one another, something passed between them spiritually.

As James blinked slowly in weariness the fox had vanished by the time his lashes parted again, but strangely, there were no prints left by the animal in the newly scattered snow. Just the ghostly outlines of snowdrops flickering in the night breeze.

Into Spring

This time Fandanzel headed North-North East. His friend would be waiting for him. The snow, now gone, had paved a silky way, dampened by the thaw.

Nuthatches busied in the still russet hedgerows of the beech, and in stark contrast to them, he thought there were three Golden Eagles, unusually circling the summit of Tegg's Nose.

Nervously, he kept a close eye on their distance to ensure they did not see him, though in fact they were simple buzzards. Fandanzel's imagination was running away with him in his anxious state of mind.

He trudged through the melting spring snow to the gate in the wall that would take him across the field; the sheep were murky and greyish, but there were daffodils beaming at him, lighting the pathway to remind him that warmer days were coming.

He climbed and clambered the rocks, using his acute sense of smell to track his progress in the right direction, darting the sodden patches of bog, acid smelling with the peat from the ancient moorland. In a few weeks would come the Cotton Grass.

The sight of deep green reed tips on the moorland immediately told him that the ground beneath was wet and boggy,

"Be wary not to get stuck Fandanzel", he muttered out loud to himself. He thought back again to the Cotton Grass; often fatal to small animals, on a windy day when all cannot be seen by blinding folly. Then the femme fatal grass- like clusters giggle away on the breeze to colonise in new areas, unaware of their blinding beauty.

He remembered losing his way the previous summer when he was a small cub, discovering the world for the first time.

He knew that there would be tension. They had not met for what seemed like an age. Their last encounter had not been straightforward, he reminded himself. Startled, instantly by a large Raven with its deep croaking sound, it flew overhead bringing him into the present world away from his thoughts.

The bird's combination of wing, tail shape and its deep call, made him aware that this was the way ahead. Ravenswood was high in the hills, the birds' nests high in the tree tops of larch, oak, and silver birch. This Raven was nesting early.

Serena was free again, her silky form was midnight blue in the midst of a late February day, whilst the naked trees and Tegg's stark reflection, gave depth to her inky pools that rippled translucently.

The sky was steel grey over the hills threatening more torrential rain. A pair of Great Crested Grebes looked stately in the reflection of the water, their slender, love-struck, and beautiful forms remarkable in their courtship display.

Spring was not far away he had decided, for he knew the signs and sounds of early spring; his master had taught him well. His master knew beauty. Afterall he had been a famous poet.

Fandanzel was tiring; there was still a long way to go before he would meet Fabian. Foxes are by nature swift, yet all too often fall prey to mankind. He had seen slower beasts taken out all too often when their wits had been down.

His biggest predator was mankind, who saw him as a threat to their livestock and as vermin, when they scavenged for food in the villages and towns.

Already there was someone on his tail waiting to catch him, and had been all his life, and he came with an army of likeminded others.

Fabian, his trusty friend, had fled to higher ground from the Cheshire Plain where his ancestors had been involved in what was named the Hunt.

Apparently this had been a terrifying experience according to his grandfather, who had been a lucky fox and escaped the thundering hooves of horses and barking of the beagles.

Fabian had taken refuge behind the outbuildings of an Inn eventually, after days of trekking easterly towards the Pennines where he had met Fandanzel for the first time whilst he had taken flight from the possible hunt...

However, his refuge was about to be short lived, Fandanzel needed to see him; they needed shelter from the rampaging fox hunters that threatened to terminate their very existence.

Trapping, poisoning or shooting had been foxs' plights for hundreds of years. The fox is not an evil creature, they just do what nature bred into them and often that meant destroying a farmer's whole free-range chicken farm costing the man his livelihood.

This man was in no mood for it to happen again. This man would track down that fox once and for all. His name was Ed Canton. The foxes had destroyed an entire chicken coop, cost him half his pheasant chicks, and terrorised the pregnant ewes on his land.

Ed Canton took a shot gun out of his locked cabinet, placed a threadbare cap upon his head and with his hound in tow, began his one man hunt for the fox, and set out the farmhouse kitchen door in search of justice.

The door slammed shut; Canton adjusted his jacket collar to fend off the icy wind, shrugged, and paced quickly through the donkey paddock towards Ridgegate reservoir, heading for the forest, gun breached beneath his arm.

A fellow farmer in the village had tipped him off that there had been sightings of a fox or two heading over to Forest Chapel, and Canton was hot on their trail.

Canton did not get any further than the Inn at Ridgegate after twenty minutes at a steady pace, the weather turned foul, sleet poured, and the wind turned to a fierce gale. He could wait. Afterall in this weather, soon his prey would be forced to lower ground to survive by scavenging in the bins of the cottages, and then the fox would fall nicely into his trap.

He buried his hands deep into his pockets and looked skywards at the falling snow.

2.

School had finished again. Where had time gone since those days shortly after Christmas, late into the winter holidays? Alex pondered.

Now it was an early Easter, and Alex, his family, along with James' family, were all due to spend the weekend at Merton Grange for Aunty Jayne and Paul's wedding.

"Wicked" he cried out and punched the air proclaiming that this Easter was going to be amazing. It had been days since he had seen James, and they needed to get their heads together for the forthcoming overnight camp and hike with the Duke of Edinburgh programme.

This year they were going to be doing their first award; Alex wanted to sleep under the stars much to the frustration of his bossy leader who always spouted on about rules, regulations and doing things by the way they were in the book.

Alex turned his mind to the present; Merton Grange was but truly historic. Adventures were to be had searching for hidden passages into the night when parents and hotel guests, staff and the likes had long retired for their slumbersome night.

A graceful Grey Heron took an impaling, rapid stab with its powerful bill at one of the Carp in the hotel pond, a stark reminder that nature was as quick to take as it was to give; the silvery orange scales were soon whisked out of sight beneath the black streaking of the Heron's front, caught firmly in its bright yellow bill, heading to the sanctuary near the Ranger Station.

The female Grey Heron had suffered badly during the harsh winter, and could not find food readily during those bleak months to feed her now greedy hatches.

The wedding party gasped at the sight in semi-horror and hastily turned to their champagne cocktails. Alex was getting bored reading the order of service card and traced the date with his forefinger, 23rd March 2002.

Did they really have to waste time at the dull wedding when they could be out on their bikes? He mused, and perched himself on the edge of a timber lawn chair, his chin cupped in his hands and watched the graceful canal boat whilst waiting for James to arrive.

He was late; Alex was getting cross and so decided to wander indoors to get a drink, gazing at the narrowboat smoothly gliding along the water in the distance, feeling the thrill of sailing it maybe one day.

3.

School had finished again. Where
It was unusually dimmer than he
remembered, inside the former
mansion and, incredibly much cooler
than outside. The air was heavy, with
the smoke from what, all Alex could
think of, a fire burning somewhere in
the room, and his eyes became
adjusted to the gloom.

It appeared, that candles were
fastened to the walls, and there was a
straw like carpet beneath his feet, he
felt sure that he heard the guttural
noise of an animal.

This was one heck of a theme for a
wedding, Alex thought to himself,
straight back to an Elizabethan
banquet; his stomach made a loud

groan, in anticipation of what was looking to be a real feast after the wedding.

He sensed that he was not alone. Voices, male and hushed came from somewhere behind him; he could not see a thing, it was as though he needed glasses, it was dark and blurred; he felt as though his head was full of cottonwool, yet almost as clear as day he heard the scraping of chairs on a timber floor followed by a hushed silence. Out of the darkness came the voice.

" Gentlemen, I, William Lloyd, Mayor of Macclesfield, stand before ye, here to address Charles, of Gawsworth, Richard of Davenport and Edward of Bramall, Thomas of Ridge and the people gathered before me of the town. By the will of the late Sir Broughton, Lord Mayor of

London, I hereby inform you that within his last will and testament he left certain money wherewith to found and endow a school in our town of Macclesfield...

..."You gentleman shall be appointed trustees this twenty second day of March 1502." Alex felt that he was in a dream, it was not 1502, it was 2002, and he had seen the date on the order of service hadn't he? Of course this was a dream,

"But, why do I feel cold and hungry? I never feel physical things in sleep" he ventured... this is really happening.

"To find and hold a priest" the voice went on "clever in grammar, and prayers are to be offered for the souls of himself and his relatives, and also for the souls...." It continued.

This, he decided, must be one of the founders of the College that was part of some great university, Alex was a witness to here, yet 500 years earlier addressing the committee; his form tutor had explained this to his class when Alex had joined juniors and met James.

His senior school's library had been named in his memory, when it had been built hundreds of years ago. Alex's head was spinning.

"This is spooking me "he cried out loud "It's like I'm re-living history". An unfamiliar voice came from directly to his left; he spun around

"Steady on lad! It's only a public bar, and you shouldn't even be at it". An older man announced, holding an empty glass and looking cross. There in a flash, he found himself stood in front of the public bar in 2002, staring at a guy in his early twenties.

"Do you want ice with it mate?" the young man asked. Where was James when he needed him, he will never believe this one, thought Alex in a stunned silence forgetting that he had ordered a coke only seconds before. Yet he had been back in 1502 for hours, so he thought.

The thoughts of spending the night under this historic haunted roof, roaming the halls looking for secret passageways and tunnels, suddenly seemed less appealing. James would be disappointed to learn that due to his best friend's ghostly encounter,

Alex Parks, of Sommerford was going home tonight to sleep in his own bed after this wedding. Even if he had to walk the fifteen miles alone.

Years later Alex recounts the story to his own children. Though for years, he never spoke a word to another breathing soul about that afternoon.

Into Mid-Summer Solstice

The packing list for the forthcoming mid- summer Bronze award of The Duke of Edinburgh Organisation, that James and Alex had signed up to do, lay unread on James' bedside table.

He would look at it sometime. Probably the day before just to double check that he had everything. He was looking forward to it; he and Alex would have a great time with the rest of the troop doing bush craft, tent pitching and staying up late.

There were only three days to go, if only they didn't have to go to school, James thought out loud and sighed.

2.

Fabian had been on time, and despite having travelled several miles, he had kept his word and met Fandanzel. Soon he was in the safety of the hills, so he thought, away from the dangers of the possible hunting.

He spent several weeks on the moors, and the days had been short, the nights long, and bitterly cold. Often he was painfully hungry, but Fandanzel had warned him that they could not take the risk of going back to the farm or the village.

It would have been fatal. They agreed to remain on the moors and scavenge.

Foxes by nature prefer to hunt alone and tend not to work as packs, and so, the two beasts often spent time apart scavenging for worms, rodents, insects and birds. Only the hedgehog remained safe with its needle like spikes; the clever little beasts would curl up when threatened and so were to their predator, simply an invincible weapon-like ball...but not for long; soon, sadly the hedgehog was to face serious population loss.

Why mankind was so intolerant of the fox, Fandanzel could not understand, surely with them keeping the rodents at bay, it would aid the so called 'Ecological Cycle' which was so precious to humans.

During June both foxes were aware of one another, but as with all their species they preferred to work alone usually by moonlight. There was food in abundance and water, and so they could relax for a few months without the need to go to lower ground in search of refuse, or the chicken coop.

For the first time in a long while, Fandanzel started to relax; he was a red fox, sporting a thick wiry reddish brown coat, almost feline with his vertically slit eyes, and retractable claws, yet his sharp muzzle and bushy red brown tail tipped with white, were characteristic of a typical fox of his breed and canine looking.

Fabian had felt compelled to meet with Fandanzel, as he had worked his way over Alderly Edge, through Gawsworth, and East to Sutton; then heading further uphill to Langley.

He had heard on the grapevine from other foxes that the farmers there were in revolt against the breed, and intended to cull any in their path. Fandanzel had helped Fabian when he had escaped the flushing of the woods in Gawsworth a year ago.

The pheasant breeders had wanted the foxes away from their chicks. He had owed his friend the warning.

As the time went on, Canton had become impatient. There was no sign of the fox, months had passed. Despite there being no recent attacks on his livestock, and him not having a grudge to bear, he was irked by the thoughts that a mere fox could have outwitted him, and he wanted his sweet revenge.

For a second time, he paced through the donkey paddock with the balmy summer's evening breeze in his beard, shirt sleeves rolled with his hound.

He paced towards his prey upon the hillside with his shotgun. The dog would lead him to the beast at last, and, once and for all he could rest.

Fandanzel and Fabian would be wise to keep their wits about them; they had dropped their guard in the beauty of the warm summer, believing them free from harm, and able to live out their days in peace.

They were blissfully unaware that danger was just at the other side of the hill, and heading straight past the ranger station, to where they basked in their belief of sanctuary.

3.

The Duke of Edinburgh Award hike and camp was imminent. James scanned the programme in his hot hand, and realising that he was about to walk 30km in a weekend, carrying an 11kg backpack, leapt out of bed, and shot to the cupboard under the stairs.

He began flinging his boots up the hall, in search of the tent and six tent pegs. He would be in his team with Alex and several others, shadowed by the leaders.

"This is going to be awesome Berry, shame you can't come, still I'll take you on a really cool walk soon, just you, me, and Dad. I won't lose you this time, and I'll prove to dad that I

can map read and I'm not as daft
with a compass as he thinks I am",
muttered the boy to his snoring
Labrador.

The route was set to take them part
of the same route, they were hoping
to take that fateful day back in
January, when they had run into
Darl.

There would be wardens on the route and checkpoints, first aid and water too, so they would at least be safe, and could just get on with having a good time thought James.

The day commenced early, each team was given a location and name. Their equipment was checked rigorously by the leaders, and as the day panned out, the boys passed through various manned checkpoints, and at each they were given an activity to carry out.

They were heading to Gradbach near the village of Flash, and then over part of the Three Shires Valley, down to where their winding patrols were also going.

The day and evening proved long, and with a painful sprained ankle that Lucy, their friend nursed, until her mum came to collect her; all in all

James and Alex went without incident.

As the first of the Duke of Edinburgh trekkers crossed the bridge over the reservoir, they hit the field where all the children were to camp for the night, the moon rose.

They were incredibly late, and would have to make pace to get their tents erected.

The leaders were anxious, and expected to have been having supper with their young charges well before this hour. Speedily they worked, every hand to the tents, to have them erect, and have a full, accounted for, group of young folk inside.

They worked efficiently to get all fed, settled, and in sleeping bags, ready for the arduous day ahead in the morning.

Most of the troop had settled by just after 12.30 a.m, their inane chatter fading sleepily with yawns, and defiant nods, very soon, children plus leaders alike were in complete slumber, apart from James and Alex.

For what they saw and heard that night could only be described as modern-day myth, fable, call it what you will. In the early hours of a June morn, as the moon boasted her full beam, there came a man heading towards them. His torch all a glow, and, with the silhouette of a cocked shotgun beneath a muscular arm.

Alex and James froze in their spot where they sat on a fallen tree; they should have been asleep and certainly not out of the tent. They decided to investigate by following the shadow away into the night that was heading towards Standing Stone.

4.

Nearby, in half moonlight standing upon a jutting rock formation were two foxes; calm in their stance, they froze still as one human paced through the wood directly towards them.

Canton was on a mission. As the barn owls hooted, the light summer's night wind echoed through the dense thickets of spruce.

The man gained speed, and torch in hand, he advanced upon four hauntingly beautiful silhouettes, two of boys, two of fox- like shadows casting into the inky depths of the top reservoir, their reflections teasingly casting jilted flickers on the tiny waves in the darkness.

The wind caressed the forest, as each twin couple, human and fox alike, unaware of each other existing only metres away from one another, looked at the approaching figure, in stunned and petrified silence.

Within a second, a long tiresome echo boomed, and the sound of gun-fire errupted. It was a ricochet of shock, bouncing from tree to tree. It echoed violently through the forest.

The deer ran north to the safety of the higher ground. The foxes knew that the best place to hide was under the Ranger's four wheel drive parked at Standing Stone, but that was nearly two miles away.

The sound of gunfire was close by. The man was shooting at anything, obviously unaware for the moment of where his prey was.

Both boys and foxes ran in the same direction unknowingly, running, panting, chests aching with strain they ran faster darting the invisible trees.

Four of them darted the pathways and, plummeting hills to the tiny wayward stream. Their feet and paws were sodden, two became four quickly, four became two, and two became one until every ounce of breath each took was in rhythm.

It was as though they became one mighty force to survive being hunted by a menacing bully, they knew nothing of. James and Alex fled downhill, Alex losing his hat but there was no way that he was stopping to pick it up.

Two boys, two foxes, a farmer and a hound stopped abruptly, skidding to a premature halt on the carpark at

Standing Stone at 1.35 a.m. It was mid-summer and yet the air was freezing, dank and silent. Fandanzel saw his breath in the cool air, and Alex's feet skidded upon what he felt was ice, but how could it be in June?

As the distant sound of the Duke of Edinburgh group leaders could be heard racing to find the boys, there appeared a ghost. Out of thin air rose the figure, smoke-like and still, just as Canton raced towards the group.

He fired his gun wildly, whilst James, Fandanzel, Alex and Fabian ran for cover amongst the ear shattering noise.

Canton's back was to an oak that the ghost was behind. It was opaque with a feint look of a man, a youngish man with what looked like old fashioned period clothing. The mist blended with the shining apparition and hovered above, illuminating the Pine trees.

The bulk of Canton was chiseled against the inky black of a summer's night. As each human and fox, turned towards one another in slow, slow motion, it was obvious whom the more scared being was.

"Where's yer troosers" came the whispering and eerie voice of the ghost of Robbie Burns. He observed Canton who had clearly remembered his shotgun, cap and hound, but was visibly only clad in his underpants, socks and walking boots. He had been taking a premature release of his bladder only moments before against a tree.

Robbie Burns was not only a famous poet, socialist and romantic figure, he had also been a farmer, and knew what fair play was about;

he had watched Canton's actions for a long time, and disapproved of his treatment to the wild foxes, especially Fandanzel. For this particular fox was the reincarnation of his own faithful dog.

As Robbie had been dying in 1759, at the young age of thirty seven, his trusted companion had lain at his side.

Now that Robbie was a ghost, he was not able to appear to Fandanzel, but he used his powers to frighten Canton to within an inch of his life. The cumbersome bulk of Canton's frame could be seen racing back towards whence he came.

Two boys held their sides laughing at a strange man without trousers, hurtling downhill as though he had seen a ghost.

Fandanzel and Fabian, cast in the moonlight, looked down the valley and observed the human spectacle. Then they blinked, stretched in unison, and curled up behind the drystone wall oblivious to what was happening.

Two somber faced leaders, complete with full beamed torches sped over the hillside to discover James and Alex open-mouthed, roaring with laughter, as one odd looking man holding a pair of trousers and a hound, with its tail between its legs, ran like wildfire away into the night.

The rest is history; needless to say that the farmer ran for his life, his quest for revenge was soon gone, for his life depended upon racing homeward away from the ghost that had tormented him.

Slipping in the mud past the water treatment works he scrambled, cap in hand, his gun long left behind. Never, in his fifty or so years had he witnessed a ghost, two foxes, and two somewhat shrieking men in one night.

5.

The camp fire was still giving out some heat, as the recently covered embers glowed and James, Alex and their leaders sat beside it, faces lit in the reflection.

A pious looking youngish chap named Justin looked on with an affronted stare; his knees pressed together balancing a note book and pen. He was wearing full-length button-up to the neck pajamas, and a checked dressing gown drawn tight by a piece of rope and neatly secured with a huge safety pin.

Evidently he had not appreciated being woken in the middle of the night. He chewed his nails whilst he patiently listened to the senior leader explaining that the boys had behaved irresponsibly.

However, James and Alex were in high spirits and so their leader's words fell on deaf ears, as the morning sun rose over the moors ready to start part two of their outdoor experience, Justin leading the way yawning and glowering.

Into Mid-Winter Solstice

With news spreading to the foxes' world that Canton had left the area; the post- worker on the lane had been told to redirect the mail to an address in Scotland, and the village oracle, a German shepherd dog, had let word out to the hills that Fandanzel would be safe, at least from Canton.

They could return to come to lower ground to scavenge for the winter that was fast approaching.

Soon Fandanzel would be making the journey west and back to civilisation; he needed to wait until the bonfires and fireworks had ceased, and be in the den by the woods, before first frost and snow, at the rear of the cottages in Langley.

There it was sheltered, and he could prey on discarded food in the bins.

Fabian had made his way to Wildboarclough, and settled, making a den by the Clough stream, in an uprooted maple tree a couple of weeks ago.

Fandanzel had witnessed Robbie, and he felt calm as though it had been fate that his enemy and master should both appear at the same time that eerie night back in summer.

The memory of that would stay with the fox for the remainder of his days. He had not seen his master since 1759. Though Robbie, by rights of a ghost, should not have appeared to Fandanzel.

The bond between man and dog all those decades ago had been immense. Fandanzel had seen

Robbie, yet Robbie and he, could not communicate.

Unexpectedly, the snow fell earlier than the Met Office had forecast, shortly after Langley had held its annual bonfire and firework display.

The ground had frozen solid almost overnight; it had been the same for ten days with little sign of letting up. Fandanzel was cold and hungry, dehydrated and lonely. He needed to get to Langley woods to make his den; it was so near and yet to a weakened fox, so far.

As he trudged over the top of the forest, head down against the oncoming strong wind, there in the distance was a light shining. A light in the forest had to be a good sign, and so, feeling his adrenalin rush, Fandanzel used all his strength to investigate. He knew that where there was light was habitation by humans, and that in turn meant food, water and warmth.

After what seemed like a long time zigzagging the snow covered rush beds on the bog, he reached the drystone wall that encased where the light was glowing from. It was St. Stephen's church, a chapel dating back hundreds of years.

The oak door at the front was open a little, just enough for him to sneak inside the candle lit room full of polished pews, and more importantly, seek out warmth and shelter; maybe food and water.

Once inside Fandanzel scurried towards another door, opening to where he could sense food, his snout working hard to locate the exact place.

There were humans, not many, they did not see him. He entered the second room that served as the chapel vestry; it was chilly, moreover, outside had felt warmer. One moment the room was lit brightly, the next it was pitch-black; a loud thud and the sound of a key turning meant only one thing.

The humans had locked up ready to go home, their laughter and chatting faded, the temperature fell and whatever he had smelled, in terms of food a few minutes ago, was about to leave the building, and not be returning until next Sunday with fresh bread for communion.

2.

Sunday December 15th dawned crisp, bright and clear. Only ten days to Christmas, and school was out for the holidays. James knelt on his bed and rubbed the condensation off the window panes above him.

Today was definitely a sledging day, and he needed to convince his dad, that it was the best thing a thirty eight year old Golf Club manager could do on his first day off for three weeks.

All James needed to do, was find a way of getting him away from his book in the lounge, and roaring fire where his dad lay; one hand holding a paperback and the other invisible inside a bag of cookies.

Berry's ears were cocked up at the rustling of the paper bag, and she stared hard willing the contents to reach her by the hearth.

After some negotiation, and James offering to clean his dad's car, make him, and mum's breakfast in bed tomorrow, and promise to tidy his bedroom. James, Berry, and his dad were heading in the car to the hills and Forest Chapel where the sledging would be awesome.

Mum had been happy to stay home and trim the tree for Christmas, and told them to have a great time. She would see them later with hot chocolate and warm scones waiting for when they got home.

There were quite a few people at the car park at Standing Stone, so James' dad suggested they park there and take a short stroll over the top where it was a little quieter.

He had been told by one of his fellow Scout leaders, at their meeting on Friday, that there was a particularly good sledging route further up the lane to the right of them.

James knew what his dad's short strolls were, and often it was a good trek, so he inwardly digested a sigh, and, trudged behind hands thrust into his pockets, looking down at his wellington boots.

Spinning, whooshing and darting they sped, hitting lumps of frozen sodden bog at about twenty five miles per hour. Spruces shot past, the air was icy and exhilarating.

James sat behind his dad holding on tight to the back of the man's jacket, who was behaving like a teenager, whooping and shrieking with the joy of a man let out for a day without boundaries.

James laughed as Berry disappeared rolling into the snow, she loved falling off the sled, and had done so years ago as a puppy. This time instead of racing in tow, she stopped and sniffed the air, trotting, she retraced her steps in a zigzag pattern, snout to the ground, tail wagging madly.

James and his dad gradually drew to a halt and hopped out of the sledge.

"Same again lad, right! I'll race you back to the church there, first one to the gate can ride up front, Go!" and off shot the recycled teenager, that was James' dad. James ran after him.

By the time they reached the church gate, Berry was there first and barking quickly, balancing on her back legs as she tried to see what was behind the window.

She had caught the scent of something exciting, and wanted to follow her instinct to find out more. She would not be distracted, no matter how hard her owners pleaded with her to.

"Stop that dreadful noise, come for a biscuit, catch, fetch..." nothing would stop her.

Some kind looking people came out of the church where they were decorating the Christmas tree, pews, and alter, in readiness for Christmas, after their afternoon gathering. James' dad was appologising for Berry's unusual behavior, when she slipped his grip, and lunged past the parishioners head first down the church, straight towards a closed oak door where she skidded.

Then again she began barking madly, and scratching at the door with her front paws. James turned to his dad. He sensed something behind the door, mystical, drawing him.

"Dad, get one of those people to open the door, please" begged James.

"No! James just put her on the lead, and between us we'll carry her to the car" replied dad.

"Dad, trust me, I have to get to whatever is behind this door, can't you see, Berry can sense something's wrong" urged James. Dad reluctantly negotiated the opening of the door with a smiling middle-aged lady, who seemed to take all afternoon with the huge bundle of keys, trying each one in turn.

James lunged past Berry, drawn to the corner of the dark room, with just enough light from the setting December sun, paling through a small window. There, huddled for warmth on a discarded hassock, barely breathing was a fox fighting for its life. Its eyes opening slightly and looking upwards into James's face, James heard it.

"Master, master, you have come, please sir, save me" came, the voice that only James could hear.

"I'm here" replied James "and I will".

A tall man with large hands, named Leonard, knelt before the fox; his eyes were kind as they gazed down at the little bundle dying in front of him.

"I'm afraid this one's not going to make it" he sadly announced to the onlookers, who murmured words of prayer. " Seen this sort of thing many times, I used to farm these hills and meadows, down at Wildboarclough, this little fella's not eaten or drunk for nearly a week, and is suffering from hypothermia. "

James pushed past the group and flung himself to the floor next to the man, who moved over. James, placed his hands over the fox, bent forward and whispered.

"I am here my faithful companion of olden days, your master, Robbie." With that James breathed over the body of the beast, and kept doing so until the brush of Fandanzel's tail began to twitch. The icy room grew warmer, soft golden light filtered through the window, and the sound of feint classical music could be heard. Though there was no-one playing it, the organist had left the church earlier. The room seemed to come alive.

When satisfied that there was enough life in the fox, James swiftly wrapped him in his coat, and slowly walked out of the building. The onlookers were puzzled, all but one, the man with the big hands and kind eyes. He turned to his wife and said

"Dora, this one'll make a good leader one day and crackin' farmer".

3.

James released Fandanzel back into the wild on Burn's Night, at the end of January. He had nursed the fox in the garden shed, researched from wildlife experts how to look after him, and been a dedicated aid in his former faithful pet's life.

More than two hundred years had altered nothing. James, the reincarnation of Robbie Burns, set Fandanzel free into the night air by the woods. He had transported him in the neighbour's cat carrier.

The night was cold, and upon the air could be heard the ceildh band playing after the Burn's Night celebrations at the Scout and Guide H.Q.

Fandanzel slipped out of the carrier quietly. He had not been afraid of the moment to go back to the wild. It was the right thing to do in his and James' minds.

In the distance an owl hooted, and Fandanzel heard the unmistakable cries of the vixen, and her mating call. With one more backward glance both boy and beast regarded one another.

"Until we meet again, wee fox, until we meet again" James quietly added into the night air, as Fandanzel braced himself to cross the frozen reservoir, Serena, to investigate the luring cry of the vixen through the farm gate, and into the dusky moonlight.

Epilogue

Eight years later after working together on The Duke of Edinburgh Awards, Bronze, Silver and moving into Gold. Alex and James went on to the World Challenge Expedition to Borneo, and climbed Kinabalu having trekked for nearly five weeks in the jungle.

The mountain is the pinnacle point of Kinabalu Park, Malaysia's First World Heritage Site, which conserves one of the richest assemblages of biological diversity, and spectacular natural landscapes in tropical Southeast Asia.

Evidently they learnt excellent survival skills with Scouts and later the Maori Explorer Scouts, Duke of

Edinburgh Awards and The World Challenge Organisation.

James went on to study a Geography Degree at Aberystwyth University, and Alex went to Glasgow to study a Physiotherapy Degree, they remained friends for the rest of their lives. Alex's passion for history was abruptly dampened by the assumed ghostly experience at the Manor.

Neither boy ever talked of their ghostly experiences to one another. After all friends they may be, but male pride had to be respected.

About the Author

Sarah McNaught spent many years working for several publishing houses throughout the U.K. She lives in Cheshire, happily married with her husband and son, who partly lives away at University.

A change of career path took her to working within schools, as a play-worker and classroom assistant, before setting up as a freelance writer and publishing consultant.

She is currently working on her next book and events organising in various sectors of the community.

Whilst enjoying writing, she also is an avid illustrator, walker and reader.

Her new book, Hamble, based upon the lives of hedgehogs, is to follow later in the year with a very different twist to the norm. However this new tale, still offers young readers the opportunity to understand nature and the countryside from the hedgehog's perspective.

Dedication

This book is dedicated to the teams of people that work voluntarily, to provide extracurricular activities, in order to enhance the lives of young people, outside of home and school. Their tireless energy and dedication to making what is a truly special opportunity, is inspirational.

With grateful appreciation to the people involved within the Scout and Guiding fraternity within Sutton, Langley, and indeed the County, The Duke of Edinburgh Award Scheme, The World Challenge Organisation, and a whole host of groups, and organisations throughout the churches of the locality, whose youth groups also provide a stable framework; a list that would be too long to be all encompassing.

With grateful acknowledgement to the wonderful people associated with the Cheshire East Council Countryside Ranger Service, whose enthusiasm for their work, and pride of the beautiful landscape inspired me; thanks to my good friends especially the three 'J's', Jane, Janice and Jenny, for patience and encouragement through the months of listening to me and editing the work; Cameron for giving me the time patience and support to create my ambition and Chris for allowing me to take over his room whilst away at University. With much appreciation to Pauline at the publishers, who made the minefield of publishing seem more like a meadow. Also Mavis for the help with illustrating and Aunt-like support. Lastly, but certainly not least, thanks to my trusty companion, Bonnie the

Labrador, whose paws were exercised for months during the research period of Fandanzel the story.

... In respectful memory of the late Cyril Dawson; local historian of Langley, author and artist.

1906-1999 ...